Rainbow of Colors

Oh every day is a rainbow of colors,
colors all around us.
Yes every day is a rainbow of colors,
colors everywhere.

Show me something red now,
like a fire engine red now.
Do you see something red now?
Point to something red.

Do you see something yellow now,
like a banana so yellow now?
Do you see something yellow now?
Whoa . . . point to something yellow.

3

Show me something blue now,
like the sky so blue now.
Do you see something blue now?
Point to something blue.

Do you see something green now,
like the grass so green now?
Do you see something green now?
Whoa . . . point to something green.

5

Oh every day is a rainbow of colors, colors all around us.
Yes every day is a rainbow of colors, colors everywhere.

Show me something white now,
like the snow so white now.
Do you see something white now?
Point to something white.

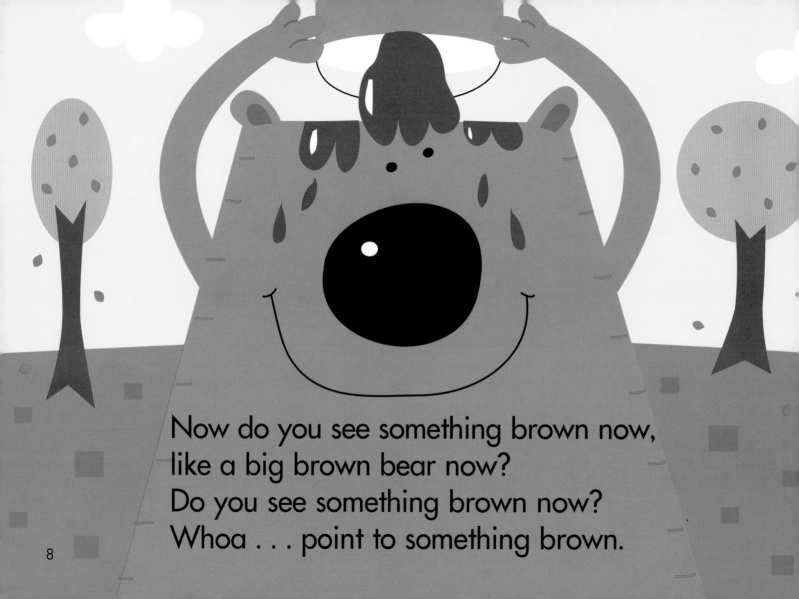

Now do you see something brown now,
like a big brown bear now?
Do you see something brown now?
Whoa . . . point to something brown.

8

Now show me something orange now,
like a pumpkin so orange now.
Do you see something orange now?
Point to something orange.

9

Do you see something black now,
like the night so black now?
Do you see something black now?
Whoa . . . point to something black.

10

Oh every day is a rainbow of colors, colors all around us.
Yes every day is a rainbow of colors, colors everywhere.

Oh every day is a rainbow of colors,
colors everywhere.